GOODNIGHT, HOCKEY FANS

Written by Andrew Larsen

Illustrated by Jacqui Lee

Kids Can Press

"Goodnight, kiddo," the boy's mom says, tucking him in.

"Can't I stay up and watch the rest of the game?" he asks. "What if I can't fall asleep?"

"Don't worry," says his dad. "You will."

With a flick of the light switch,
the boy's room turns quiet. So quiet
it seems to roar.

The boy waits until the roar slowly
fades, then listens.

He listens to the whistling wintry
wind outside.

He listens for the sounds of the game
on the television in the other room.

What if I can't fall asleep? he worries.

Snug beneath the covers, the boy reaches for his flashlight.
He shines it at the posters of his favorite players.

He shines it at the pennant
of his favorite team.

He shines it at the moon
peeking through the curtains.

He shines it at the puck
on the shelf.
"Goodnight, hockey puck,"
he whispers.

He takes out his dad's old radio from under his pillow.

With a gentle click, he turns it on and moves the dial ... slowly, slowly.

Station to station.

Past the music.

Past the talking.

Past the hush.

And then he hears it.

"*Welcome back, hockey fans from coast to coast,*" says the familiar voice. "*What a game we have tonight!*"

The boy closes his eyes and settles in.
He shifts.
He listens to the voice on the radio.
He drifts ...

"The home team wins the face-off in their own end.

They move the puck along the boards.

Stickhandling around the defensemen, they pass it up the ice.

"*There's a quick shot on the net.*

Oh!

What a save by the goalie!

*The rebound goes into the corner as both
teams scramble for the puck!*

"What's this?

This is amazing, hockey fans!

A boy has skated onto the ice —

It looks like he's going after the puck.

"He's got it!

He's got the puck.

He's picking up speed.

He's whistling like the wind.

He is flying!

"He winds up.

He shoots —

"He scores!"

"What a play!
What a goal!
What a game!"

The boy smiles in his sleep as the cheering crowd slowly fades into the quiet of his room.

The boy's parents look in on him.

"Sweet dreams, champ," they whisper
from the doorway.

And then they hear it.

They hear the voice from the radio tucked
under their sleeping boy's pillow.

"Goodnight, hockey fans,"
says the voice. "Goodnight,
hockey fans from coast to coast."